W9-CYZ-583

BOONIE

Freedom Runner

by DEBORAH BURGGRAAF

Illustrated by SHAUN HOWARD

Deborah Burggraaf
1.16.16

PROTECTIVE HANDS
Communications
Riviera Beach, Florida

dburgg.com

ISBN 978-0-9845161-5-5
Library of Congress Control Number 2010940161

Published
By
Protective Hands Communications
Riviera Beach, FL 33404
Toll free: 866-457-1203
www.protectivehands.com
info@protectivehands.com

Printed in the United States of America

To Willem, whose love for dogs inspired this story.

Forever lives Sky, Boonie, Monsoon and Puddles.

D. B.

To Sharon Howard, my Mother, with love.

S. H.

With wooden crutches against the wall,
Timmy did stand but three feet tall.

Since birth, Little Timmy could not walk;
he crawled and balanced as he talked.

As he stood at only three,
Boonie, his best friend was at his knee.

From the window, Lil' Timmy would watch
Boonie run outside in the hot, Florida sun.

Across his cheek a tear would drop
because Little Timmy wanted to run and hop.

Boonie would splash through ponds with frogs,
past Ibis and Blue Heron and even wild hogs.

One day, Lil' Timmy wiped his cheek.

He reached for his crutches and went out for a peek.

The opened door warmed Timmy's face
and Boonie stayed near and did not race.

Side by side, the two walked outside.
'Ole Boonie kept up with an even stride.

The two best friends wanted to explore and see
the Cypress, Palms and Melaleuca trees.

With grass grazed with dew in the heat of the day,
they were delighted to be out and simply to play.

Past the pond, Timmy walked to visit Dapper, the duck.
"Quack, quack," Dapper called, "You are in luck!"

"Today is the day we are given to play
in the warmth of the sun on this glorious day."

Dapper fluttered his feathers and oiled his wings.
"Minny moe, minny moo, quackadack diddly dee,
today is the day; it's all about me!"

Dapper and Timmy and Boonie they walked,
laughing and splashing through tall, marshy stalks.

Nearby, an Ibis family was searching for bugs
and Boonie reached out for an afternoon hug.

The three plopped down under a shady oak tree.
They took sips of water as Boonie refreshed with glee.

Timmy wiped his face with a red bandana
and kept Boonie cool at his neck, a real Montana.

Off the three went to a nearby canal.
Timmy hobbled — a real trooper who would not fail.

With a little snack bag from Timmy's backpack,
the three sat down for an afternoon snack.

An apple, banana and grapes with cheese,
Dapper quacked, "Yummy, may I have a little more, please?"

The canal sparkled with life! There were chirping birds and tall trees.
Sweet songs softly swept across the field of greens.

"Minny moe, minny moo, quackadack diddly dee,
today is the day; it's all about me!"

Just then a Black Racer slithered on past
their afternoon lunch, but did not move fast.

The snake slowly swayed from side to side
and slithered on by them with an even, smooth glide.
“Wow!” Lil’ Tim shouted. “How beautiful he is!”
Boonie barked his soft bark with a wide grin.

After lunch near the water, Timmy reached for his crutches
to stand near a tree, rough bark to his touches.
The morning sun turned gray with white, puffy clouds.

Timmy stood by his best friend, tall and proud.
“Minny moe, minny moo, quackadack diddly dee,
today is the day; it’s all about me.”

Timmy looked to the sky to see a break in the clouds
and started to cry out real loud,

"I think I can walk with one, not two.
These crutches I have just will not do."

As Timmy felt a raindrop on the top of his shoulder,
he dropped one wooden crutch next to a boulder.

Boonie stood by his leg as if a soft prop.
Lil' Timmy stood upright; his knees did not pop.

Tall he stood waving with his one arm now free
to the crow who cawed from above, “You stand tall just like me.”

“You can do it, you can soar! Keep your legs on your walk.”
Boonie stared. Dapper watched. Not a soul even talked.

As the black crow flew away in flight,
Timmy's second crutch dropped, as if out of sight.

"Minny moe, minny moo, quackadack diddly dee,
today is the day; it's all about me!"
Timmy took his first steps without wooden sticks.
Boonie by his side, he did not move quick.

“Look Boonie, I can stand and walk tall in the grass!”

“Let’s move slowly, I can do it, I can slowly stride past
the fields of green grass and out to the canal
and back to our home without feeling so frail.”

In the summer sprinkles from above, the three ventured out.
No umbrella, no sun, just the warmth of Boonie's snout.

Lil' Timmy kept walking and he would not stop.
He glanced to see little bunnies run, skip and hop.

After looking at the Red-bellied turtles on the water's edge
they could still see the house surrounded by the hedge.

"We should head back home," Dapper clacked with glee.
Boonie barked his soft bark and he did agree.

With slow steps Timmy walked past the Black Racer and trees
to the home that was safe and which welcomed the three.

Past the wooden crutches that now lay on the ground,
new legs for Timmy were finally found.
“Minny moe, minny moo, quackadack diddly dee,
today is the day; it’s all about me.”

"Believe in yourself and remember, never give up!"
"I did it! You can too!" cheered Timmy, hugging his pup.

Boonie jumped up to lick Timmy's joyful face.
Dapper clacked out, "Come now, let's not race!"

By himself, Timmy walked proud and tall.
With Boonie nearby, he would not fall.

Slowly, the three approached the red, house door,
Lil' Timmy took a deep breath and said once more,
"Minny moe, minny moo, quackadack diddly dee,
today is the day; it *was* all about me."

THE END

Deborah Burggraaf's second picture book tells the tale of her Black and Tan Coonhound Dog, Boonie. After reading an article about how helpful these types of dogs are with disabilities, Deborah wrote her story which shows Boonie's desire to be free, while at the same time demonstrating his unconditional dedication toward his loved ones.

Deborah Burggraaf resides in Palm Beach County, Florida, where she is a middle school teacher.

Shaun Howard's use of vibrant watercolor combined with ink brings each character to life. Shaun's mastery of skill with each stroke of the brush allows children to become active participants in this delightful story exemplifying that dreams do come true.

Shaun Howard received his Bachelor's Degree in Fine Arts from Morgan State University in Baltimore, Maryland. Shaun lives in Atlanta, Georgia with his family.

Thank you for reading **Boonie: FREEDOM RUNNER**. Please visit our website: **www.dburgg.com**. You will find lots of fun exercises on our website. We look forward to hearing from you.

Deborah Burggraaf

Email: deb@dburgg.com
Phone: 561-429-6733